D0127041

To my mother, Pauline,
who taught me how to sing,
and my father, Aubrey,
who taught me how to plant peas.
—D.M.

For Eitan, a wonderful friend
and gardener, with a green thumb.
—O.E.

Inch by Inch
The Garden Song
Text originally published as lyrics of song entitled "Garden Song"
copyright © 1975 by Cherry Lane Music Publishing, Inc.
Illustrations copyright © 1995 by Ora Eitan
Manufactured in China. All rights reserved.
For information address HarperCollins Children's Books,
a division of HarperCollins Publishers,
195 Broadway, New York, NY 10007.

Library of Congress Cataloging-in-Publication Data
Mallett, David.
  Inch by inch : the garden song / by David Mallett ; pictures by Ora
Eitan.
       p.   cm.
  Summary: Inch by inch, row by row, a child grows a garden with the
help of the rain and the earth. Based on a popular folk song.
  ISBN 0-06-024303-1. — ISBN 0-06-024304-X (lib. bdg.)
  ISBN 0-06-443481-8 (pbk.)
  1. Folk songs, English—Texts. [1. Gardening—Songs and music.
2. Folk songs.] I. Eitan, Ora, date, ill. II. Title.
PZ8.3.M3104In 1995   93-38352
[E]—dc20   CIP
                                                              AC

Typography by Christine Hoffman Casarsa
❖
14 15 16 SCP 20 19 18 17 16 15 14 13
First Harper Trophy edition, 1997

Inch by Inch
The Garden Song

by David Mallett • pictures by Ora Eitan

HarperCollinsPublishers

Inch by inch, row by row,
gonna make this garden grow.

All it takes is a rake and a hoe
and a piece of fertile ground.

Inch by inch, row by row,
someone bless these seeds I sow.

Someone warm them from below
till the rain comes tumblin' down.

Pullin' weeds

and pickin' stones,

we are made of dreams and bones.

Feel the need to grow my own

'cause the time is close at hand.

Grain for grain, sun and rain,
find my way in nature's chain.

Tune my body and my brain
to the music from the land.

Plant your rows straight and long,

temper them with prayer and song.

Mother Earth will make you strong

if you give her love and care.

Old crow watching hungrily

from his perch in yonder tree.

In my garden I'm as free

as that feathered thief up there.

Inch by inch, row by row,
gonna make this garden grow.

All it takes is a rake and a hoe
and a piece of fertile ground.

Inch by inch,
row by row,
someone bless
these seeds I sow.
Someone warm
them from below
till the rain comes
tumblin' down.

Inch by Inch
The Garden Song

by David Mallett

Moderately

Inch by inch, row by row, gon-na make this
Inch by inch, row by row, Some-one bless these

gar-den grow, ___ All it takes is a rake and a hoe and a
seeds I sow, ___ Some-one warm them from be - low 'til the

1. piece of fer-tile ground.

2. rain comes tum-bl-in' down.

Fine

Pull- in' weeds and pick - in' stones, ___ man is made of
Plant your rows ___ straight and long, ___ tem- per them with